Mrs. Malory and a Time to Die